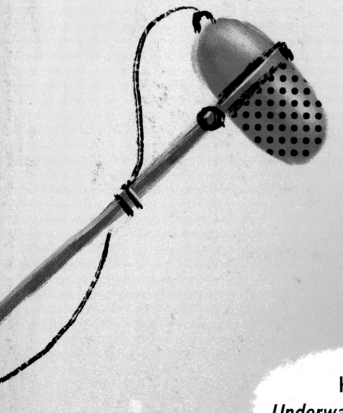

E
DYCKMAN

MAY '18

. . . 1 . . .
Hey! Who did this?!

For Owen
and Daniel.
–S.M.

For Chris,
aka Big Meanie.
(But maybe he's just
misunderstood.)
–A.D.

Text
copyright
© 2018 by Ame
Dyckman
Illustrations copyright
© 2018 by Scott
Magoon

$17.99

All rights
reserved. Published by
Orchard Books, an imprint of Scholastic
Inc., *Publishers since 1920.* ORCHARD BOOKS and
design are registered trademarks of Watts Publishing
Group, Ltd., used under license. SCHOLASTIC and associated
logos are trademarks and/or registered trademarks of Scholastic
Inc. • The publisher does not have any control over and does not
assume any responsibility for author or third-party websites or their
content. • No part of this publication may be reproduced, stored in a
retrieval system, or transmitted in any form or by any means, electronic,
mechanical, photocopying, recording, or otherwise, without written
permission of the publisher. For information regarding permission, write to
Scholastic Inc., Attention: Permissions Department, 557 Broadway, New
York, NY 10012. • This book is a work of fiction. Names, characters,
places, and incidents are either the product of the author's
imagination or are used fictitiously, and any resemblance to
actual persons, living or dead, business establishments,
events, or locales is entirely coincidental.
Library of Congress Cataloging-in-
Publication Data available

ISBN
978-1-338-11247-4
• 10 9 8 7 6 5 4 3 2 1 •
18 19 20 21 22 • Printed in China
38 • First edition, May 2018 •
The text type was set in Chelsea
Market and Adrianna Condensed.
Book design by Jess
Tice-Gilbert

MISUNDERSTOOD SHARK
Starring SHARK!

Written by Ame Dyckman

Illustrated by Scott Magoon

Orchard Books
New York
An Imprint of Scholastic Inc.

"Sharrrk!
The people are watching!
Don't eat that fish
in front of the people!"

"You misunderstood! I wasn't gonna eat him.

I was just . . ."

"Fun Fact about that! Sharks can grow and lose 30,000 teeth in their lifetime."

Can I faint now?

30,000?!

Shark's Tooth Fairy must be EXHAUSTED!

"Fine, Shark. Maybe you weren't going to eat that fish . . ."

"Shark?"

"Where's Shark?"

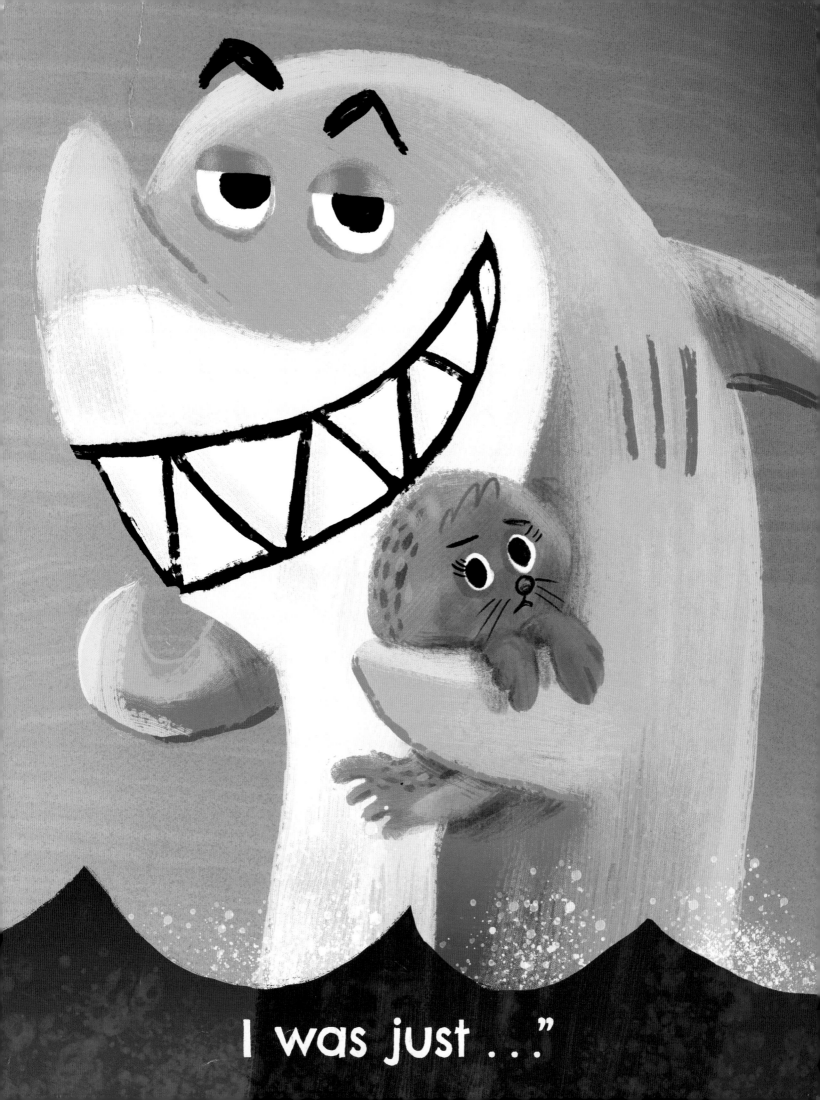

"I was just ..."

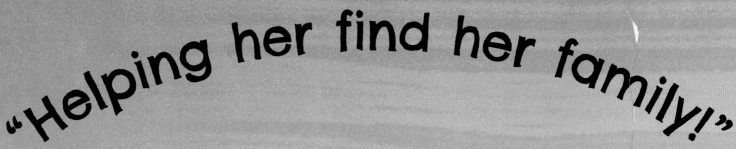

"Fun Fact about that! A great white shark can eat 22,000 pounds of food in a year . . . and seals are their favorite."

"People, I MAY have misunderstood Shark!"

"Shark?"

"Where's Shark NOW?!"

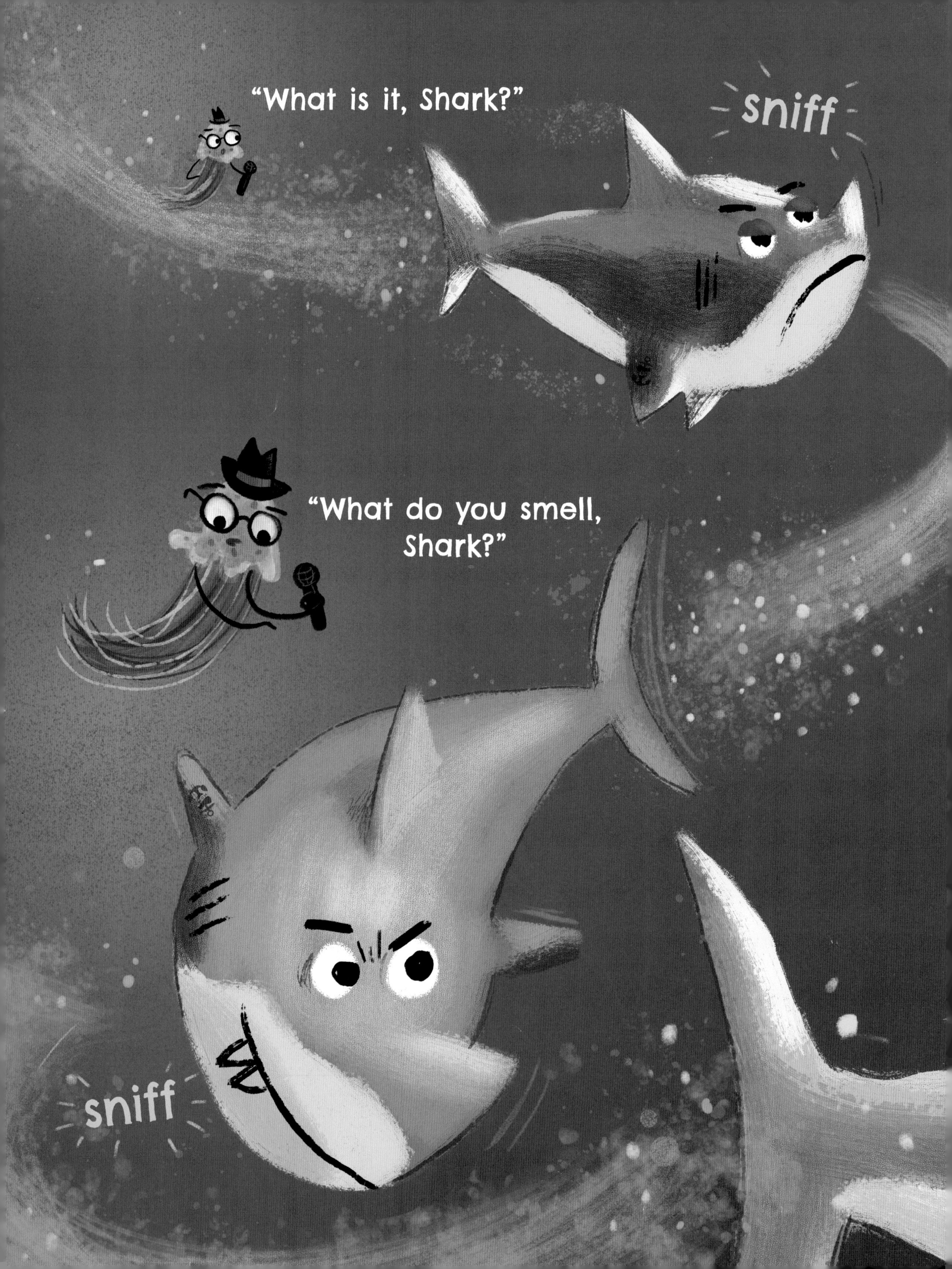
"What is it, Shark?"
sniff
"What do you smell, Shark?"
sniff

“Tell us what you smell,
Shark!”

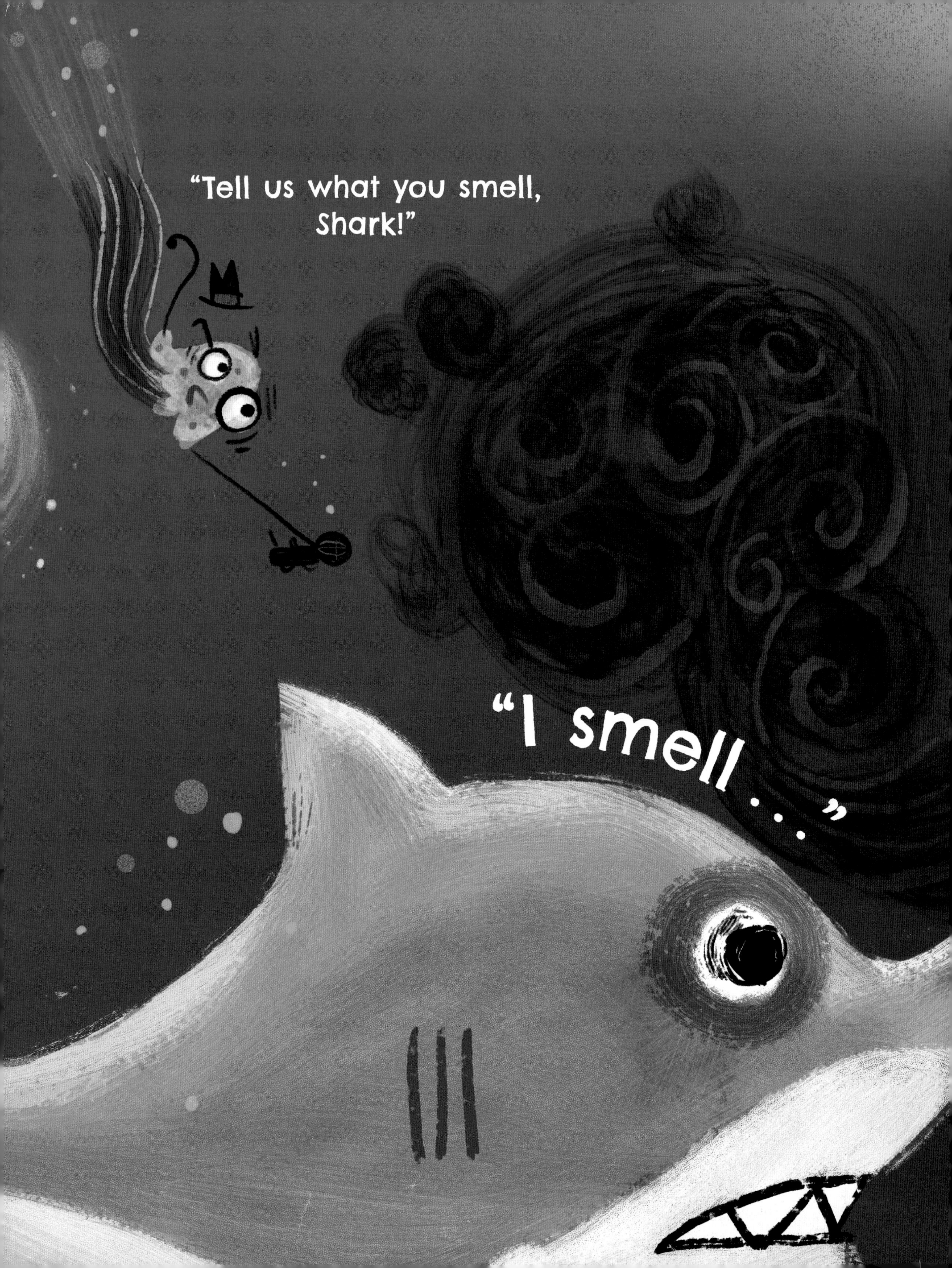

“I smell . . .”

"OH! Fun Fact about that! Some sharks can smell a single drop of blood in a million drops of wa—"

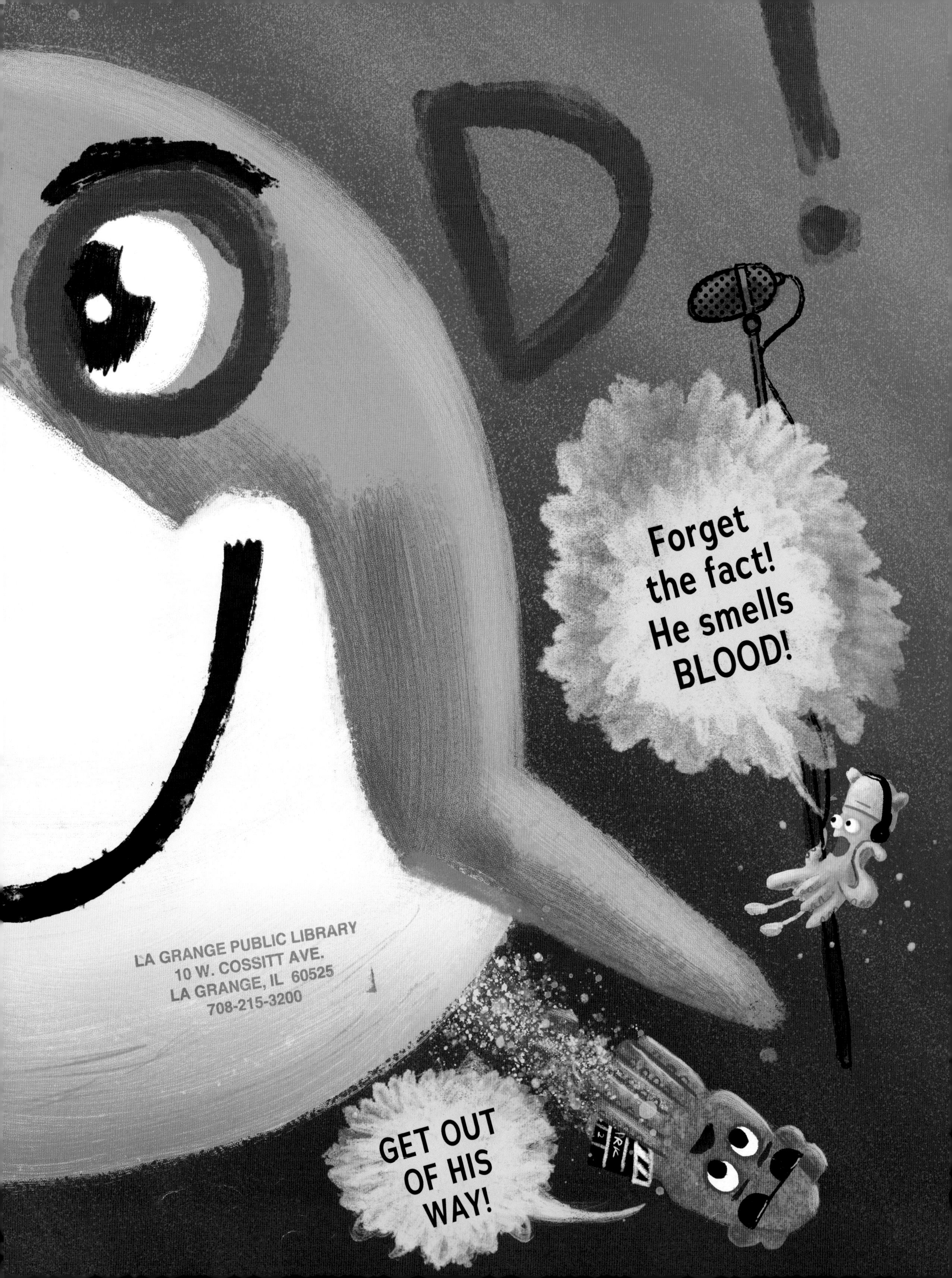
D!
Forget the fact! He smells BLOOD!
GET OUT OF HIS WAY!

"Nooo, Shark!
Don't eat the people—
IN FRONT OF THE PEOPLE!"

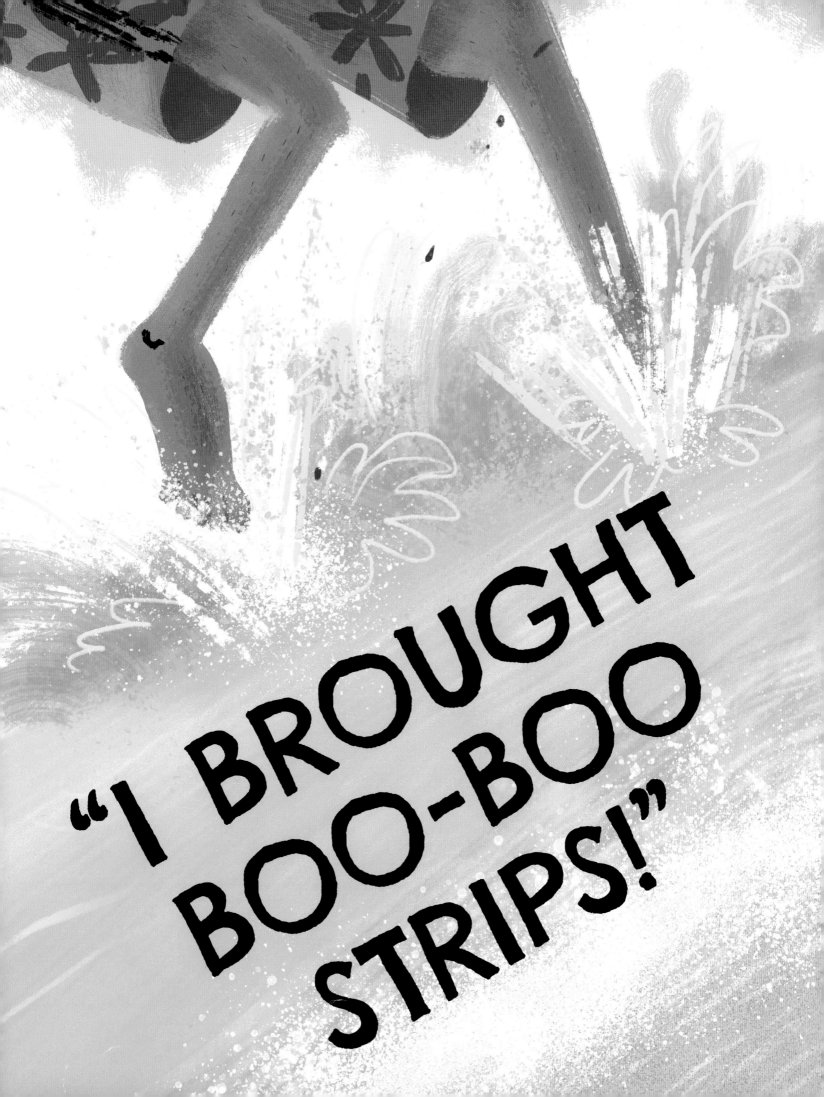

"And there you have it, folks. Sharks really are . . . just misunderstood!"

GULP!
dab dab dab
You ate me! I can't believe you REALLY ate me!
IN FRONT OF THE PEOPLE!
SHARK

"Playing hide-and-seek with you!"

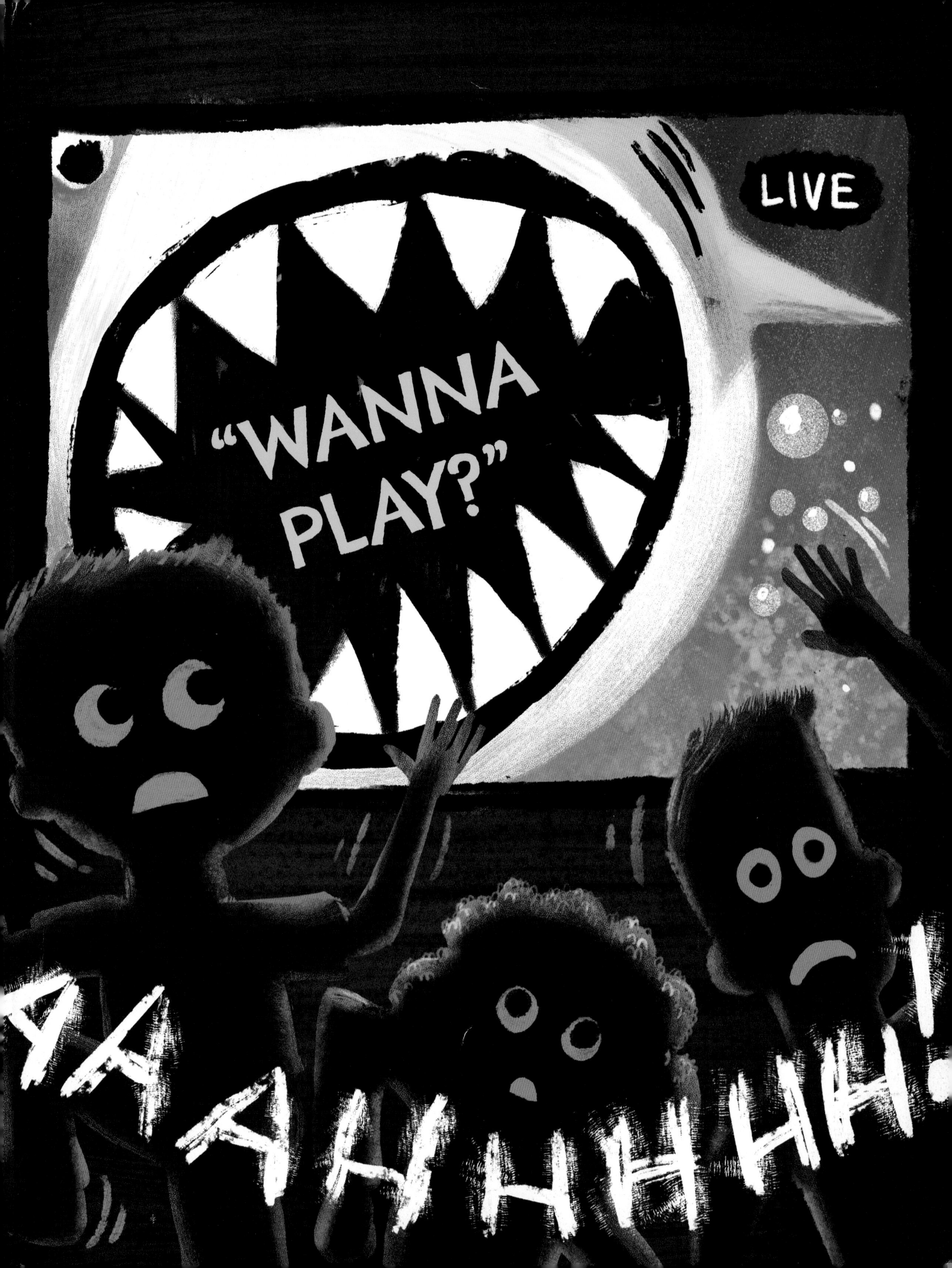
LIVE
"WANNA PLAY?"
AAAHHHHH!